Estelle M. Hurll

The madonna in art

A mother is a mother still- The bodiest thing alive

Estelle M. Hurll

The madonna in art
A mother is a mother still- The bodiest thing alive

ISBN/EAN: 9783741188961

Manufactured in Europe, USA, Canada, Australia, Japa

Cover: Foto ©Andreas Hilbeck / pixelio.de

Manufactured and distributed by brebook publishing software
(www.brebook.com)

Estelle M. Hurll

The madonna in art

THE MADONNA IN ART

Art Series

THE MADONNA IN ART
Estelle M. Hurll.

CHILD LIFE IN ART
Estelle M. Hurll.

ANGELS IN ART
Clara Erskine Clement.

LOVE IN ART
Mary Knight Potter.

L. C. PAGE AND COMPANY
(INCORPORATED)
196 Summer Street, Boston, Mass.

Madonna of Castelfranco

Photogravure from the Painting by Giorgione in the
Parish Church, Castelfranco

THE
MADONNA IN ART

BY

ESTELLE M. HURLL

Illustrated

A mother is a mother still —
The holiest thing alive.
—COLERIDGE.

BOSTON
L. C. PAGE AND COMPANY
(INCORPORATED)
1898

Colonial Press :
Electrotyped and Printed by C. H. Simonds & Co.
Boston, Mass., U. S. A.

CONTENTS.

ILLUSTRATIONS.

ILLUSTRATIONS.

ILLUSTRATIONS.

PREFACE.

THIS little book is intended as a companion volume to " Child-Life in Art," and is a study of Madonna art as a revelation of motherhood. With the historical and legendary incidents in the life of the Virgin it has nothing to do. These subjects have been discussed comprehensively and finally in Mrs. Jameson's splendid work on the " Legends of the Madonna." Out of the great mass of Madonna subjects are selected, here, only the idealized and devotional pictures of the Mother and Babe. The methods of classifying such works are explained in the Introduction.

Great pains have been taken to choose as illustrations, not only the pictures which are universal favorites, but others which are less widely known and not easily accessible.

The cover was designed by Miss Isabelle A. Sinclair, in the various colors appropriate to the Virgin Mary. The lily is the Virgin's flower, *la fleur de Marie*, the highest symbol of her purity. The gold border surrounding the panel is copied from the ornamentation of the mantle worn by Botticelli's Dresden Madonna.

ESTELLE M. HURLL.

New Bedford, Mass., May, 1897.

INTRODUCTION.

IT is now about fifteen centuries since
the Madonna with her Babe was first
introduced into art, and it is safe to say
that, throughout all this time, the subject has been unrivalled in popularity.
It requires no very profound philosophy
to discover the reason for this. The
Madonna is the universal type of motherhood, a subject which, in its very nature,
appeals to all classes and conditions of
people. No one is too ignorant to understand it, and none too wise to be superior to its charm. The little child
appreciates it as readily as the old man,
and both, alike, are drawn to it by an ir-
resistible attraction. Thus, century after

century, the artist has poured out his soul in this all-prevailing theme of mother love until we have an accumulation of Madonna pictures so great that no one would dare to estimate their number. It would seem that every conceivable type was long since exhausted; but the end is not yet. So long as we have mothers, art will continue to produce Madonnas.

With so much available material, the student of Madonna art would be discouraged at the outset were it not possible to approach the subject systematically. Even the vast number of Madonna pictures becomes manageable when studied by some method of classification. Several plans are possible. The historical student is naturally guided in his grouping by the periods in which the pictures were produced; the critic, by the technical schools which they represent. Besides these more scholarly methods, are others, founded on

simpler and more obvious dividing lines.
Such are the two proposed in the following pages, forming, respectively, Part I.
and Part II. of our little volume.

The first is based on the style of composition in which the picture is painted;
the second, on the subject which it treats.
The first examines the mechanical arrangement of the figures; the second asks,
what is the real relation between them?
The first deals with external characteristics; the second, with the inner significance.

Proceeding by the first, we ask, what
are the general styles of treatment in
which Madonna pictures have been rendered? The answer names the following
five classes:

1. The Portrait Madonna, the figures
in half-length against an indefinite background.

2. The Madonna Enthroned, where

the setting is some sort of a throne or dais.

3. The Madonna in the Sky or the "Madonna in Gloria," where the figures are set in the heavens, as represented by a glory of light, by clouds, by a company of cherubs, or by simple elevation above the earth's surface.

4. The Pastoral Madonna, with a landscape background.

5. The Madonna in a Home Environment, where the setting is an interior.

The foregoing subjects are arranged in the order of historical development, so far as is possible. The first and last of the classes enumerated are so small, compared with the others, that they are somewhat insignificant in the whole number of Madonna pictures. Yet, in all probability, it is along these lines that future art is most likely to develop the subject, choosing the portrait Madonna because of its universal adaptability, and representing the Madonna in her home, in an effort to realize, historically, the New Testament scenes. Of the remaining three, the enthroned Madonna is, doubtless, the largest class, historically considered, because of the long period through which it has been represented. The pastoral and enskied Madonnas were in high favor in the first period of their perfection.

Our next question is concerned with the aspects of motherhood displayed in Madonna pictures: in what relation to her child has the Madonna been represented? The answer includes the following three subjects:

1. The Madonna of Love (The Mater Amabilis), in which the relation is purely maternal. The emphasis is upon a mother's natural affection as displayed towards her child.

2. The Madonna in Adoration (The

Madre Pia), in which the mother's attitude is one of humility, contemplating her child with awe.

3. The Madonna as Witness, in which the Mother is preëminently the Christ-bearer, wearing the honors of her proud position as witness to her son's great destiny.

These subjects are mentioned in the order of philosophical climax, and as we go from the first to the second, and from the second to the third, we advance farther and farther into the experience of motherhood. At the same time there is an increase in the dignity of the Madonna and in her importance as an individual. In the Mater Amabilis she is subordinate to her child, absorbed in him, so to speak; his infantine charms often overmatch her own beauty. When she rises to the responsibilities of her high calling, she is, for the time being, of equal interest and importance.

Æsthetically, she is now even more attractive than her child, whose seriousness,
in such pictures, takes something from
his childlikeness. Chronologically, our list
reads backwards, as the religious aspect
of Mary's motherhood was the first treated
in art, while the naturalistic conception
came last. Regarded as expressive of national characteristics, the Mater Amabilis
is the Madonna best beloved in northern
countries, while the other two subjects belong specially to the art of the south.

It will be seen that any number of
Madonna pictures, having been arranged
in the five groups designated in Part I.,
may be gathered up and redistributed in
the three classes of Part II. To make this
clear, the pictures mentioned in the first
method of classification are frequently referred to a second time, viewed from an
entirely different standpoint. Since the
lines of cleavage are so widely dissimilar

in the two cases, both methods of study are necessary to a complete understanding of a picture. By the first, we learn a convenient term of description by which we may casually designate a Madonna; by the second, we find its highest meaning as a work of art, and are admitted to some new secret of a mother's love.

PART I.

MADONNAS CLASSED BY THE STYLE OF COMPOSITION.

THE MADONNA IN ART.

CHAPTER I.

THE PORTRAIT MADONNA.

THE first Madonna pictures known to us are of the portrait style, and are of Byzantine or Greek origin. They were brought to Rome and the western empire from Constantinople (the ancient Byzantium), the capital of the eastern empire, where a new school of Christian art had developed out of that of ancient Greece. Justinian's conquest of Italy sowed the new art-seed in a fertile field, where it soon took root and multiplied rapidly. There was, however, little or no improvement in the type for a long period; it remained practically unchanged till the thirteenth century. Thus, while a Byzantine Madonna is to be found in nearly every old church in Italy, to see one is to see all. They are half-length figures against a background of gold leaf, at first laid on solidly, or, at a somewhat later date, studded with cherubs. The Virgin has a meagre, ascetic countenance, large, ill-shaped eyes, and an almost peevish expression; her head is draped in a heavy, dark blue veil, falling in stiff folds.

Unattractive as such pictures are to us from an artistic standpoint, they inspire us with respect if not with reverence. Once objects of mingled devotion and admiration, they are still regarded with awe by many who can no longer admire. Their real origin being lost in obscurity, innumerable legends have arisen, attributing them to miraculous agencies, and also endowing them with power to work miracles. There is an early and widespread tradition, imported with the Madonna from the East, which makes St. Luke a painter. It is said that he painted many portraits of the Virgin, and, naturally, all the churches possessing old Byzantine pictures claim that they are genuine works from the hand of the evangelist. There is one in the Ara Coeli at Rome, and another in S. Maria in Cosmedino, of which marvellous tales are told, besides others of great sanctity in St. Mark's, Venice, and in Padua.

It would not be interesting to dwell, in any detail, upon these curious old pictures. We would do better to take our first example from the art which, though founded on Byzantine types, had begun to learn of nature. Such a picture we find in the Venice Academy, by Jacopo Bellini, painted at the beginning of the fifteenth

century, somewhat later than any corresponding picture could have been found
elsewhere in Italy, as Venice was chronologically behind the other art schools.
The background is a glory of cherub
heads touched with gold hatching. Both
mother and child wear heavy nimbi, ornamented with gold. These points recall
Byzantine work; but the gentler face of
the Virgin, and the graceful fall of her
drapery, show that we are in a different
world of art. The child is dressed in a
little tunic, in the primitive method.

With the dawn of the Italian Renaissance, the old style of portrait Madonna
passed out of vogue. More elaborate
backgrounds were introduced from the
growing resources of technique. In the
fifteenth and sixteenth centuries, pictures
of the portrait style were comparatively
rare. Raphael, however, was not above
adopting this method, as every lover of

JACOPO BELLINI. — MADONNA AND CHILD.

the Granduca Madonna will remember.
His friend Bartolommeo also selected
this style of composition for some of the
loveliest of his works.

The story of the friendship between
these two men is full of interest. At the
time of Raphael's first appearance in
Florence (1504), Bartolommeo had been
four years a monk, and had laid aside,
apparently forever, the brush he had previously wielded with such promise. The
young stranger sought the Frate in his
cell at San Marco, and soon found the
way to his heart. Stimulated by this
new friendship, Bartolommeo roused himself from lethargy and resumed the prac-
tice of art with increasing success. It
is pleasant to trace the influence which
the two artists exerted upon each other.
The older man had experience and learn-
ing; the younger had enthusiasm and
genius. Now it happened that, by na-

ture, Bartolommeo was specially gifted in the arrangement of large composi- tions, with many figures and stately ar- chitectural backgrounds. It is by these that he is chiefly known to-day. So it is the more interesting that, when Raphael's sweet simplicity first touched him, he turned aside, for the time, from these elaborate plans and gave himself to the portrayal of the Madonna in that simplest possible way, the half-length portrait pic- ture. Several of these he painted upon the walls of his own convent, glorifying that dim place of prayer and fasting with visions of radiant and happy motherhood. One of these may still be seen in the cell sometimes called the Capella Giovanato. It instantly recalls the Tempi Madonna of Raphael, both in the pose of the figure and in the genuineness of feeling ex- hibited. Damp and decay have warred in vain against it, and the modern visitor lingers before the Mother and Babe with hushed admiration.

Two other similar frescoes have been removed to the Academy. They show the same motherly tenderness, the same innocent and beautiful babyhood. The mother holds her child close in her arms, pressing her forehead to his, or bending her cheek to receive his kiss. He throws his little arm about her neck, clinging to her veil or caressing her face.

Besides this group of pictures by Bartolommeo, there are other scattered instances of portrait Madonnas during the Italian Renaissance, by men too great to be tied to the fashions of their day. Mantegna was such a painter, and Luini another. All told, however, their pictures of this sort make up a class too rare to deserve longer description.

A century later, the Spanish school occasionally reverted to the same style of treatment. A pair of notable pictures are the Madonna of Bethlehem, by Alonzo Cano, and the Madonna of the Napkin, by Murillo. Both are in Seville, the latter in the museum, the former still hanging in its original place in the cathedral.

Of Cano's work, a great authority[1] on Spanish art has written, that, "in serene, celestial beauty, it is excelled by no image of the blessed Mary ever devised in Spain." Murillo's picture is better known, and has a curious interest from its history. The cook in the Capuchin monastery, where the artist had been painting, begged a picture as a parting gift. No canvas being at hand, a napkin was offered instead, on which the master painted a Madonna, unexcelled among his works in brilliancy of color.

As the portrait picture was the first style of Madonna known to art, so, also, it

[1] Stirling-Maxwell, in " Annals of the Artists of Spain."

GABRIEL MAX. — MADONNA AND CHILD.

is the last. By a leap of nearly a thousand years, we have returned, in our own day, to the method of the tenth century. It is strange that what was once a matter of necessity should at last become an object of choice. In the beginning of Madonna art, the limited resources of technique precluded any attempts to make a more elaborate setting. Such difficulties no longer stand in the way, and where we now see a portrait Madonna, the artist has deliberately discarded all accessories in order better to idealize his theme.

Take, for instance, the portrait Madonnas by Gabriel Max. Here are no details to divert the attention from motherhood, pure and simple. We do not ask of the subject whether she is of high or of low estate, a queen or a peasant. We have only to look into the earnest, loving face to read that here is a mother. There are two pictures of this sort, evidently studied from the same Bohemian models. In one, the mother looks down at her babe; in the other, directly at the spectator, with a singularly visionary expression. When weary with the senseless repetition of the set compositions of past ages, we turn with relief to a simple portrait mother like this, at once the most primitive and the most advanced form of Madonna art. It is only another case where the simplest is the best.

CHAPTER II.

THE MADONNA ENTHRONED.

N every true home the mother is queen, enthroned in the hearts of her loving children. There is, therefore, a beautiful double significance, which we should always have in mind, in looking at the Madonna enthroned. According to the theological conception of the period in which it was first produced, the picture stands for the Virgin Mother as Queen of Heaven. Understood typically, it represents the exaltation of motherhood.

In the history of art development, the enthroned Madonna begins where the portrait Madonna ends. We may date it from the thirteenth century, when Cima-

bue, of Florence, and Guido, of Siena,
produced their famous pictures. Similar
types had previously appeared in the
mosaic decorations of churches, but now,
for the first time, they were worthily set
forth in panel pictures.

The story of Cimabue's Madonna is
one of the oft-told tales we like to hear
repeated. How on a certain day, about
1270, Charles of Anjou was passing
through Florence; how he honored the
studio of Cimabue by a visit; how the
Madonna was then first uncovered; how
the people shouted so joyously that the
street was thereafter named the Borgo
dei Allegri; and how the great picture
was finally borne in triumphal procession
to the church of Santa Maria Novella,—
all these are the scenes in the pretty
drama. The late Sir Frederick Leighton
has preserved for future centuries this
story, already six hundred years old, in a

charming pageant picture: "Cimabue's
Madonna carried through the streets of
Florence." This was the first work ever
exhibited by the English artist, and was
an important step in the career which
ended in the presidency of the Royal
Academy.

Cimabue's Madonna still hangs in Santa Maria Novella, over the altar of the
Ruccellai chapel, and thither many a pil-
grim takes his way to honor the memory
of the father of modern painting. The
throne is a sort of carved armchair, very
simple in form, but richly overlaid with
gold; the surrounding background is filled
with adoring angels. Here sits the Madonna, in stiff solemnity, holding her child
on her lap. If we find it hard to admire
her beauty, we must note the superiority
of the picture to its predecessors.

For the enthroned Madonna in a really
attractive and beautiful form, we must

pass at once to the period of full art
development.   In the interval, many
variations upon the theme have been in-
vented. The throne may be of any size,
shape, or material; the composition may
consist of any number of figures. The
Madonna, seated or standing, is now the
centre of an assembly of personages symmetrically grouped about her. There is
little or no unity of action among them;
each one is an independent figure. The
guard of honor may be composed of
saints, as in Montagna's Madonna, of the
Brera, Milan; or again it is a company of
angels, as in the Berlin Madonna, attributed to Botticelli, similar to which is
the picture by Ghirlandajo in the Uffizi
Gallery. Where saints are represented,
each one is marked by some special em-
blem, the identification of which makes,
in itself, an interesting study. St. Peter's
key, St. Paul's sword, St. Catherine's

wheel, and St. Barbara's tower soon become familiar symbols to those fond of this kind of lore.

Among the idealized presences about the Virgin's throne may sometimes be seen the prosaic figure of the donor, whose munificence has made the picture possible. This is well illustrated in the famous Madonna of Victory in the Louvre, painted in commemoration of the Battle of Fornovo, where Mantegna represents Francesco Gonzaga, commander of the Venetian forces, kneeling at the Virgin's feet.

A charming feature in many enthroned Madonnas is the group of cherubs below, — one, two, or the mystic three. They are not the exclusive possession of any single school of art; Bartolommeo and Andrea del Sarto of the Florentines, Francia of the Bolognese, and Bellini and Cima of the Venetians were particularly partial to them. The treatment in Northern Italy gives them a more definite purpose in the composition than does that of Florence, for here they are always musicians, playing on all sorts of instruments, — the violin, the mandolin, or the pipe.

Bartolommeo was specially successful in the subject of the enthroned Madonna, having fine gifts of composition united with profound religious earnestness. The great picture in the Pitti gallery at Florence may serve as a typical example. Andrea del Sarto's *chef-d'œuvre* — the Madonna di San Francesco (Uffizi) — may also be assigned to this class, although the arrangement is entirely novel. The Virgin, holding the babe in her arms, stands on a sort of pedestal, carved at the corners with a design of harpies, from which the picture is often known as the Madonna of the Harpies. The pedestal

PERUGINO. — MADONNA AND SAINTS. (DETAIL.)

throne is also seen in two of Correggio's
Dresden pictures, but here the Virgin is
seated, with the child on her lap. An
exceedingly simple throne Madonna is
that of Luini, in the Brera at Milan,
where the Virgin sits on a plain coping
not at all high.

A beautiful Madonna enthroned is by
Perugino, in the Vatican Gallery at Rome;
one of the artist's best works in power and
vivacity of color. The throne is an archi-
tectural structure of elegant simplicity of
design, apparently of carved and inlaid
marble. The Virgin sits in quiet dignity,
her face bent towards the bishops at her
right, St. Costantius and St. Herculanus.
On the other side stand the youthful St.
Laurence and St. Louis of Toulouse.
Although Perugino was an exceedingly
prolific artist, he did not often choose this
particular subject. On this account the
picture is especially interesting, and also

because it is the original model of well known works by two of the Umbrian painter's most illustrious pupils.

Many, indeed, were the apprentices trained in the famous *bottega* at Perugia, but, among them all, Raphael and Pinturicchio took the lead. These were the two who honored their master by repeating, with modifications of their own, the beautiful composition of the Vatican. Pinturicchio's picture is in the Church of St. Andrea, at Perugia. A charming feature, which he introduced, is a little St. John, standing at the foot of the throne. Raphael's picture is the so-called Ansidei Madonna, of the National Gallery, London, purchased by the English government, in 1885, for the fabulous price of £72,000. The composition is here reduced to its simplest possible form, with only one saint on each side, — St. Nicholas on the right, St. John the Baptist on the left. The Virgin and child give no attention to these personages, but are absorbed in a book which is open on the Mother's knee.

Raphael had no great liking for this style of picture, which was rather too formal for his taste. It is noticeable that, in the few instances where he painted it, he took the suggestion, as here, from some previous work. Thus his Madonna of St. Anthony, also in the National Gallery (loaned by the King of Naples), was based upon an old picture by Bernardino di Mariotto, according to the strict orders of the nuns for whose convent it was a commission. The Baldacchino Madonna of the Pitti, at Florence, is closely akin to Bartolommeo's composition in the same gallery.

Glancing, briefly, at these scattered examples, we learn that the enthroned Madonna belongs to every school of Italian art, and exhibits an astonishing variety of forms. Probably it was in the North of Italy that it flourished most. The Paduan School has its fine representation in Mantegna's picture, already referred to; the Brescian, in Moretto's Madonna of S. Clemente; the Veronese, in Girolamo dai Libri's splendid altar piece in San Giorgio Maggiore; the Bergamesque, in Lotto's Madonna of S. Bartolommeo. Above all, it was in Venice, the Queen City of the Adriatic, that the enthroned Madonna reached the greatest popularity: the spirit of the composition was peculiarly adapted to the Venetian love of pomp and ceremony.

To understand Venetian art aright, we must distinguish the character of the earlier and later periods. With Vivarini, Bellini, and Cima, the Madonna in Trono was the expression of a devout religious feeling. With Titian, Tintoretto, and Veronese, it was merely one among many popular art subjects. Thus arose two different general types. The earlier Madonna was a somewhat cold type of beauty; the faultless regularity of her features and the imperturbable calm of her expression make her rather unapproachable; but she shows a strong, sweet purity of character, worthy of profound respect.

One of Cima's most important works is the Madonna of this type in the Venice Academy. High on a marble throne, she sits under a pillared portico, behind which stretches a pleasant landscape. Three saints stand on each side,—an old man, a youth, and a maiden. On the steps sit two choristers playing the violin and mandolin.

Palma's great altar-piece, at Vicenza, is another splendid enthroned Madonna. Attended by St. George and St. Lucy, and entertained by a musical angel seated at her feet, the Virgin supports her beautiful boy, as he gives his blessing.

Bellini's enthroned Madonnas are known throughout the world. The picture by which he established his fame was one of this class, originally painted for a chapel in San Giobbe, but now hanging in the Venice Academy. Ruskin has pronounced it "one of the greatest pictures ever painted in Christendom in her central art power." It is a large composition, with three saints at each side, and three choristers below.

The Frari Madonna is in a simpler vein, and consists of three compartments, the central one containing the Virgin's throne. The angioletti, on the steps, are probably the most popular of their charming class in Venice.

The San Zaccaria Madonna was painted when Bellini was over eighty

GIOVANNI BELLINI. — MADONNA OF SAN ZACCARIA. (DETAIL.)

years old, and has certain technical qualities surpassing any the artist had previously attained. The depth of light
and shade is particularly remarkable; the
colors rich and harmonious. The attendant saints are St. Lucy on the right,
a pretty blonde girl, with St. Jerome beyond her, absorbed in his Bible; opposite, stand St. Catherine, pensively looking
down, and St. Peter, in profound medita-
tion. The entire picture, both in conception and execution, may be considered
a representative example of the times.

Following the Bellini school, and forming, as it were, a connecting link between
the earlier and the later art, was Giorgione.
Less than a score of existing works give
witness to the rare spirit of this master,
who was spared to earth only thirty-four
years. These are of a quality to place
him among the immortals. The enthroned Madonna is the subject of two,

one in the Madrid Gallery, and another at Castel-Franco. They create an entirely distinct Madonna ideal,—a poetic being, who sits, with drooping head and dreamy eyes, as if seeing unspeakable visions.

The Castel-Franco picture expresses the finest elements in Venetian character. Every other composition seems elaborate and artificial when compared with the simplicity of this. Other Madonnas seem almost coarse beside such delicacy. The Virgin's throne is of an unusual height,—a double plinth,—the upper step of which is somewhat above the heads of the attendant saints, Liberale and Francis. This simple, compositional device emphasizes the effect of her pensive expression. It is as if her high meditations set her apart from human companionship. There is, indeed, something almost pathetic in her

isolation, but for the strength of character
in her face. The color scheme is as
simple and beautiful as the underlying
conception. The Virgin's tunic is of
green, and the mantle, falling from the
right shoulder and lying across her lap,
is red, with deep shadows in its large
folds. The back of the seat is covered
with a strip of red and gold embroidery.

The later period of Venetian art is
marked by a new ideal of the Virgin.
She is now a magnificent creature of
flesh and blood. Her face is proud and
handsome; her figure large, well-propor-
tioned, and somewhat voluptuous. No
Bethlehem stable ever sheltered this
haughty beauty; her home is in kings'
palaces; she belongs distinctly to the
realm of wealth and worldliness. She
has never known sorrow, anxiety, or
poverty; life has brought her nothing
but pleasure and luxury. Her throne

stands no longer in the sacred place of some inner sanctuary, where angel choristers make music. It is an elevated platform, at one side of the composition, as in Titian's Pesaro altar-piece, and Veronese's Madonna in the Venice Academy. This gives an opportunity for a display of elaborate draperies, such as we may see in Veronese's picture.

The peculiar qualities of art in Verona and Venice are blended in Paolo Veronese. No artist ever enjoyed more the splendors of color, or combined them in more enchanting harmonies. Such gifts transform the commonest materials, and, though his Virgin is a very ordinary woman, she has undeniable charms. An oft-copied figure, in this picture, is that of the little St. John, a universal favorite among child lovers.

The reader must have remarked that, though the fundamental idea of the en-

VERONESE. — MADONNA AND SAINTS.

throned Madonna is that of queenship,
the Virgin wears no crown in any of
the pictures thus far cited; the crowned
Madonna is not characteristic of Italian
art. It is found occasionally in mosaics
from the eighth to the eleventh centuries, and in some of the early votive pictures, but does not appear in the later
period except in a few Venetian pictures
by Giovanni da Murano and Carlo Cri-
velli. The same idea was often carried
out by placing two hovering angels over
the Virgin's head, holding the crown between them. Botticelli's Madonna of the
Inkhorn is treated in this way.

The crown is essentially Teutonic in
origin and character. Turning to the
representative art of Germany and Bel-
gium, we find the Virgin almost invari-
ably wearing a crown, whether she sits on
a throne, or in a pastoral environment.
No better example could be named than

the celebrated Holbein Madonna, of Darmstadt, known chiefly through the copy in the Dresden Gallery. Here the imposing height of the Virgin is rendered still more impressive by a high, golden crown, richly embossed and edged with pearls. Beneath this her blond hair falls loosely over her beautiful neck, and gleams on the blue garment hanging over her shoulders. Strong and tender, this noble figure sums up the finest elements in the Madonna art of the North.

A simple and lovely form for the Madonna's crown is the narrow golden fillet set with pearls, singly or in clusters. This is placed over the Virgin's brow just at the edge of the hair, which is otherwise unconfined. This is seen on Madonnas by Van Eyck (Frankfort), Dürer (woodcut of 1513), Memling (Bruges), Schongauer (Munich).

In the enthroned Madonna by Quen-

QUENTIN MASSYS. — MADONNA AND CHILD.

tin Massys, in the Berlin Gallery, we have
many typical characteristics of Northern
art. The throne itself is exceedingly rich,
ornamented with agate pillars with embossed capitals of gold. The Virgin has
the fine features and earnest, tender
expression which recalls earlier Flemish
painters. Her dress falls in rich, heavy
folds upon the marble pavement. But, as
with Van Eyck and Memling, Holbein
and Schongauer, fine clothes do not con-
ceal her girlish simplicity or her loving
heart. A low table, spread with food,
stands at the left,— a curious domestic
element to introduce, and thoroughly
Northern in realism.

Considered as a symbol of the exaltation of motherhood, there is no reason
why the throne should go out of fashion;
but if it is to appear, it must be used
intelligently, and with some adaptation to
present modes of thought, not servilely

imitated from the forms of a by-gone age.
This is a fact too little appreciated by the
artists of to-day. Many modern pictures
could be cited — by Bouguereau, Itten-
bach, and others — of enthroned Madonnas in which is adopted the form, but
not the spirit, of the Italian Rennaissance.
In such works, the setting is a mere
affectation entirely out of taste. If we
are to have a throne, let us have a
Madonna who is a veritable queen.

CHAPTER III.

(THE MADONNA IN GLORIA.)

WE have seen that the first Madonnas were painted against a background either of solid gold, or of cherub figures, and that the latter style of setting was continued in the early pictures of the enthroned Madonna. The effect was to idealize the subject, and carry it into the region of the heavenly. This was the germinal idea which grew into the " Madonna in Gloria."

The glory was originally a sort of nimbus of a larger order, surrounding the entire figure, instead of merely the head. It was oval in shape, like the almond or mandorla.

A picture of this class is the famous Madonna della Stella, of Fra Angelico. It is in a beautiful Gothic tabernacle, which is the sole ornament of a cell in San Marco, Florence. At every step in these sacred precincts, we meet some reminder of the Angelic Brother. How the gray walls blossomed, under his brush, into forms and colors of eternal beauty! After seeing the larger wall-paintings in corridors and refectory, this little gem seems to epitomize his choicest gifts. A rich frame, fit setting for the jewel, encloses an outer circle of adoring angels, and within, the central panel contains only the full length figure of the Virgin with her child, against a mandorla formed of golden rays running from centre to circumference. The Madonna is enveloped in a long, dark blue cloak, drawn around her head like a Byzantine veil. A single star gleams above her brow, from which

FRA ANGELICO. — MADONNA DELLA STELLA.

is derived the title of the picture. She holds her child fondly, and he, with responsive affection, nestles against his mother, pressing his little face into her neck. Faithful to the standards of his predecessors, and untouched by the new spirit of naturalism all about him, the monk painter preserves, in his conception, the most sacred traditions of past ages, and yet unites with them an element of love and tenderness which appeals strongly to every human heart.

It is but a step from this earlier form of the Madonna in Gloria to the more modern style of the Madonna in the Sky, where the field of vision is enlarged, and we see the Virgin and child raised above the surface of the earth. In some pictures, her elevation is very slight. There is a curious composition, by Andrea del Sarto (Berlin Gallery), where we are puzzled to know if the Madonna is enthroned or enskied. A flight of steps in the centre leads up as if to a throne, but above these the Virgin sits in a niche, on a bank of clouds.

In Correggio's Madonna of St. Sebastian, in the Dresden Gallery, the Virgin seems to be descending from heaven to earth with her babe, and the surrounding clouds and cherubs rest literally upon the heads of the saints who are honored by the vision.

In other pictures the dividing line between earth and heaven is much more strongly marked. We have a landscape below, then a stratum of intervening air, and, in the upper sky, the Madonna with her child. The lower part of the picture is occupied by a company of saints, to whom the heavenly vision is vouchsafed; or, in rare cases, by cherubs. The Virgin appears in a cloud of cherub heads, or accompanied by a few child - angels.

UMBRIAN SCHOOL. — GLORIFICATION OF THE VIRGIN.

There are a few pictures in which her mother, St. Anne, sits with her. Adoring seraphs sometimes attend, one on each side, or even sainted personages. All these variations are exemplified in the pictures which we are to consider.

The first has come down to us from the hand of some unknown Umbrian painter. In the National Gallery, London, where it now hangs, it was once attributed to Lo Spagna, but is now entered in the catalogue as nameless. It matters little whether or not we know the name of the master; he could ask no higher tribute to his talent than the universal admiration which his picture commands.

In the foreground of a quiet Umbrian lanscape is a marble balcony, on the railing of which sit two captivating little boy choristers. One roguish fellow pipes on a trumpet, while the other, his face tip-tilted to the heavenly vision, makes music on a small guitar. Above, on a cloud, sits the Virgin, with the sweet, mystic smile on her face, so characteristic of Umbrian art. She supports her babe with her right arm, and in her left hand carries a lily stalk. The child, standing on his mother's knee and clinging to her neck, turns his face out with sweet earnestness. In clouds at the side, tiny cherubs bear tapers, while others, floating above, hold a large crown just over her head.

Although we cannot limit this style of picture to any special locality, it appears to have found much favor in the art of Northern Italy. In the Brescian school, Moretto was unusually fond of the subject. His treatment of the theme is somewhat heavy; there is little of the ethereal in his celestial vision, either in the type of womanhood or in the style of arrangement. In defiance of the law of gravitation, he poses his upper figures so as to

MORETTO. — MADONNA IN GLORY.

form a solid pyramid, wide at the base, and tapering abruptly to the apex.

In the glorified Madonna of St. John the Evangelist, Brescia, the pyramidal effect is accentuated by curtains draped back on either side of the upper part of the composition. In the Madonna of San Giorgio Maggiore, at Verona, we have a much more attractive picture. The " gloria " encompassing the vision is clearly defined, giving so strong an effect of the supernatural that we cease to judge the composition by ordinary standards of natural law. The Virgin's white veil flutters from her head as if caught by some heavenly breeze. Her cloak floats about her by the same mysterious force, held in graceful festoons by winged cherub heads.

Below is a group of five virgin martyrs, with St. Cecilia in the centre, wearing a crown of roses; St. Lucia holds the awl, the instrument of her torture, looking down at St. Catherine, who leans against her terrible wheel; St. Agnes, on the other side, reads quietly from a book while she caresses her lamb, and St. Barbara stands behind her, with eyes lifted to the sky. They are all splendid young Amazons, recalling Moretto's fine St. Justina of the Vienna Gallery. There is no trace of ascetism in their strong, well-developed figures, and in their faces no suggestion of an unhealthy pietism.

Moretto's ideals were an anticipation of the most advanced ideas of the modern science of physical culture. His Madonna and saints derive their beauty neither from over refinement on the one hand, nor from sensuous charms on the other, but from sane and harmonious self-development.

The Berlin Gallery contains a third glorified Madonna by the same painter,

treated as a Holy Family. St. Elizabeth
sits beside the Virgin, who holds her own
boy on her right side, while bending to
embrace the little St. John with the left
arm. So large a group is not appropri-
ately treated in this way, yet the picture
is so fine a work of art as to disarm
criticism.

Still another representative of the Brescian school must be considered in the
person of Savoldo. Born of a noble
family, and following painting as an
amusement rather than as an actual
profession, his works are rare, and one
of the finest examples of his art is the
Glorification of the Virgin, in the Brera
Gallery, at Milan. The mandorla-shaped
glory surrounds the Virgin's figure, studded
with faintly discerned cherub heads. On
either side, a musical angel is in adoration; four saints stand on the earth below.
The entire conception is rendered with

the utmost delicacy: the grace and beauty
of the Madonna are of exactly the quality to make her appearance a beatific
vision.

From Brescia we turn to Verona, where
we again find many pictures of the beautiful subject.   There are, in the churches
of Verona, at least three notable works, by
Gianfrancesco Caroto, in this style.   One
is in Sant' Anastasia, another is in San
Giorgio, and the third — the artist's best
existing work — is in San Fermo Maggiore, and shows the Virgin's mother, St.
Anne, seated with her in the clouds.

Girolamo dai Libri was a few years
younger than Caroto, and at one period
was, to some extent, an imitator of the
latter.   Beginning as a miniaturist, he
finally attained a high place among the
Veronese artists of the first order.   His
characteristics can nowhere be seen to
better advantage than in the Madonna of

St. Andrew and St. Peter, in the Verona
Gallery. The Virgin is in an oval glory,
edged all around with small, fleecy clouds.
She has a beautiful, matronly face, with
abundant hair, smoothly brushed over her
forehead. The two apostles, below, are fine,
strong figures, full of virility.

Morando, or Cavazzola, was, doubtless,
the most gifted of the older school of
Verona, possessing some of the best qualities of the later master, Paolo Veronese.
We should not leave the school, therefore,
without mentioning a remarkable contri-
bution he added to this class of pictures in
his latest altar-piece. Here the upper air
is filled with a sacred company, the Virgin
and child are attended by St. Francis and
St. Anthony, and surrounded by seven
allegorical figures to represent the cardi-
nal virtues. Below are six saints, specially
honored in the Franciscan Order. The
picture is called the finest production of

the school in the first quarter of the sixteenth century.

In the Venetian school, Titian and Tintoretto both painted the subject of the Madonna in glory, but the pictures are not notable compared with many others from their hands.

From the North of Italy we naturally turn next to the South, to inquire what Raphael was doing at the same period in Rome. Occupied by many great works under the papal patronage, he still found time for his favorite subject of the Madonna, painting some pictures in the styles already mastered, and two for the first time in the style of the Madonna in the sky.

The first was the Foligno Madonna, now in the Vatican Gallery. It was painted in 1511 for the pope's secretary, Sigismund Conti, as a thank-offering for having escaped the danger of a fall-

SPANISH SCHOOL. — MADONNA ON THE CRESCENT MOON.

ing meteor at Foligno. No thoughtful
observer can be slow to recognize the
superiority of this composition over all
others of its kind in point of unity. Here
is no formal row of saints, each absorbed
in his or her own reflections, apart from
any common purpose. On the contrary,
all unite in paying honor to the Queen
of Heaven. Not less superior to his contemporaries was the painter's skill in
arranging the figures of Mother and child
with such grace of equilibrium that they
seem to float in the upper air.

In the Sistine Madonna, Raphael carried this form of composition to the
highest perfection. So simple and ap·
parently unstudied is its beauty, that
we do not realize the masterliness of its
art. We seem to be standing before an
altar, or, better still, before an open window, from which the curtains have been
drawn aside, allowing us to look directly

into the heaven of heavens. A cloud of
cherub faces fills the air, from the midst
of which, and advancing towards us, is
the Virgin with her child. The down-
ward force of gravity is perfectly coun-
terbalanced by the vital energy of her
progress forward. There is here no
uncomfortable sense, on the part of
the spectator, that natural law is disre-
garded. While the seated Madonna in
glory seems often in danger of falling
to earth, this full-length figure in motion
avoids any such solidity of effect.

The figures on either side are also
so posed as to arouse no surprise at
their presence. We should have said
beforehand that heavy pontifical robes
would be absurdly incongruous in such
a composition, but Raphael solves the
problem so simply that few would sus-
pect the difficulties. The final touch of
beauty is added in the cherub heads be-

BOUGUEREAU. — MADONNA OF THE ANGELS.

low, recalling the naïve charm of the similar figures in the Umbrian picture we have considered.

After the time of Raphael, a pretty form of Madonna in glory was occasionally painted, showing the Virgin with her babe sitting above the crescent moon. The conception appears more than once in the paintings of Albert Dürer, and later, artists of all schools adopted it. Sassoferrato's picture in the Vatican Gallery is a popular example. Tintoretto's, in Berlin, is not so well known. In the Dresden Gallery is a work, by an unknown Spanish painter of the seventeenth century, differing from the others in that the Virgin is standing, as in the oft-repeated Spanish pictures of the Immaculate Conception.

It is of pictures like this that our poet Longfellow is speaking, when he thus apostrophizes the Virgin:

" Thou peerless queen of air,
As sandals to thy feet the silver moon dost wear." '

The enskied Madonna involves many
technical difficulties of composition, and
demands a high order of artistic imagina-
tion. It could hardly be called a frequent
subject in the period of greatest artistic
daring, and no modern painter has shown
any adequate understanding of the subject, though there are not lacking those
who have made the attempt. Bodenhausen, Defregger, Bouguereau, have all fol-
lowed Raphael in representing the Queen
of Heaven as a full-length figure in the
sky; but their conception has not the
dignity corresponding to the style of treatment.

Impatient and dissatisfied with such
modern art, we turn back to the old masters with new appreciation of their great
gifts.

CHAPTER IV.

THE PASTORAL MADONNA.

T was many centuries before art, at first devoted exclusively to figure painting, turned to the study of natural scenery. Thus it was that Madonna pictures, of various kinds, had long been established in popular favor before the idea of a landscape setting was introduced. We need not look for interesting pictures of this class before the latter part of the fifteenth century, and it was not until the sixteenth that the pastoral Madonna, in its highest form, was first produced. Even then there was no great number which show a really sympathetic love of nature.

In the ideal pastoral, the landscape entirely fills the picture, and the figures are, as it were, an integral part of it. Such pictures are so rare that we write in golden letters the names of the few who have given us these treasures.

Raphael's justly comes first in the list. His earliest Madonnas show his love of natural scenery, in the charming glimpses of Umbrian landscape, which form the background. These are treated, as Müntz points out, with marked "simplicity of outline and breadth of design." They are, however, but the beginning of the great things that were to follow. The young painter's sojourn in Florence witnessed a marvellous development of his powers. Here he was surrounded by the greatest artists of his time, and he was quick to absorb into himself something of excellence from them all. His fertility of production was amazing. In a period of four years (1504-1508), interrupted by visits to

Perugia and Urbino, he produced about twenty Madonnas, in which we may trace the new influences affecting him.

Leonardo da Vinci was, doubtless, his greatest inspiration, and it was from this master-student of nature that the young man learned, with new enthusiasm, the value of going directly to Nature herself. The fruit of this new study is a group of lovely pastoral Madonnas, which are entirely unique as Nature idyls. Three of these are among the world's great favorites. They are, the Belle Jardinière (The Beautiful Gardener), of the Louvre Gallery, Paris; the Madonna in Grünen (The Madonna in the Meadow), in the Belvedere Gallery, Vienna; and the Cardellino Madonna (The Madonna of the Goldfinch), of the Uffizi, Florence.

We turn from one to another of these three beautiful pictures, always in doubt as to which is the greatest. Fortunately,

it is a question which there is no occasion
to decide, as every lover of art may be the
happy possessor of all three, in that highest mode of possession attained by devoted
study.

In each one we have the typical Tuscan
landscape, filling the whole picture with its
tranquil beauty. The " glad green earth "
blossoms with dainty flowers; the fair blue
sky above is reflected in the placid surface
of a lake. From its shores rise gently
undulating hills, where towers show the
signs of happy activity. In the foreground
of this peaceful scene sits a beautiful
woman with two charming children at her
knee. They belong to the landscape as
naturally as the trees and flowers; they
partake of its tranquil, placid happiness.

Almost identical in general style of
composition, the three pictures show
many points of dissimilarity when we
come to a closer study of the figures.

RAPHAEL. — MADONNA IN THE MEADOW.

Considered as a type of womanly beauty, the Belle Jardinière is perhaps the most commonplace of the three Virgins, or, to put it negatively, the least attractive. She is distinctly of the peasant class, gentle, amiable, and entirely unassuming. The Madonna in the Meadow is a maturer woman, more dignified, more beautiful. The smooth braids of her hair are coiled about the head, accentuating its lovely outline. The falling mantle reveals the finely modelled shoulders. The Madonna of the Goldfinch is a still higher type of loveliness, uniting with gentle dignity a certain delicate, high-bred grace, which Raphael alone could impart. Her face is charmingly framed in the soft hair which falls modestly about it. One wonders if any modern *coiffeur* could invent so many styles of hair dressing as does this gifted young painter of the sixteenth century.

Turning from the mother to the children, we find the same general types repeated in the three pictures, but with some difference of *motif*. The Christ-child of the Belle Jardinière is looking up fondly to his mother. In the Vienna picture he is eagerly interested in the cross which the little St. John gives him. In the Uffizi picture he is more serious, and strokes the goldfinch with an air of abstraction, meditating on the holy things his mother has been reading to him.

The arrangement of the three figures is the same in all the pictures, and is so entirely simple that we forget the greatness of the art. The Virgin, dominating the composition, brings into unity the two smaller figures. This unity is somewhat less perfect in the Belle Jardinière, because the little St. John is almost neglected in the intense absorption of mother and child in each other.

Once again, in the later days at Rome, Raphael recurred to the pastoral Madonna type of this Florentine period, and painted the picture known as the Casa Alba Madonna. We have again the same smiling landscape and the same charming children, but a Virgin of an altogether new order. A turbaned Roman beauty of superb, Juno-like physique, she does not belong to the idyllic character of her surroundings. It is as if some brilliant exotic had been transplanted from her native haunts to quiet fields, where hitherto the modest lily had bloomed alone.

As Raphael's first inspiration for the pastoral Madonna came from the influence of Leonardo da Vinci, it is of interest to compare his work with that of the great Lombard himself. Critics tell us that the Madonna pictures in which he came nearest to his model are the Madonna in the Meadow and the Holy

Family of the Lamb. (Madrid.) These we may place beside the Madonna of the Rocks, which is the only entirely authentic Da Vinci Madonna which we have.

It is only the skilled connoisseur who, in travelling from Paris to Vienna, and from Vienna to Madrid, can hold in memory the qualities of technique which link together the three pictures; but for general characteristics of composition, the black and white reproductions may suffice. Leonardo availed himself of his intimate knowledge of Nature to choose from her storehouse something which is unique rather than typical. The rock grotto doubtless has a real counterpart, but we must go far to find it. In the river, gleaming beyond, we see the painter's characteristic treatment of water, which Raphael was glad to adopt. The triangular arrangement of the figures, the relation of the Virgin to the children,

LEONARDO DA VINCI.— MADONNA OF THE ROCKS.

the simple, childish beauty of the latter,
and their attitude towards each other —
all these points suggest the source of
Raphael's similar conceptions. The Virgin's hair falls over her shoulders entirely
unbound, in gentle, waving ripples.

We do not need to be told, though the
historian has taken pains to record it,
that a feature of personal beauty by which
Leonardo was always greatly pleased was
"curled and waving hair." We see it in
the first touch of his hand when, as a boy
in the workshop of Verrochio, he painted
the wavy-haired angel in his Master's
Baptism; and here, again, in the Virgin,
we find it the crowning element of her
mysterious loveliness. We try in vain to
penetrate the secret of her smile, — it
is as evasive as it is enchanting. And
herein lies the distinguishing difference
between Leonardo and Raphael. The
former is always mysterious and subtle;

the latter is always frank and ingenuous. While both are true interpreters of nature, Leonardo reveals the rare and inexplicable, Raphael chooses the typical and familiar. Both are possessed of a strong sense of the harmony of nature with human life. The smile of the Virgin of the Rocks is a part of the mystery of her shadowy environment;[1] the serenity of the Madonna in the Meadow belongs to the atmosphere of the open fields.

Among others who were affected by the influence of Leonardo — and chief of the Lombards — was Luini. His pastoral Madonna has, however, little in common with the landscapes of his master, judging from the lovely example in the Brera.

[1] That the Leonardesque *smile* requires a Leonardesque *setting* is seen, I think, in the pictures by Da Vinci's imitators. The Madonna by Sodoma, recently added to the Brera Gallery at Milan, is an example in point. Here the inevitable smile of mystery seems meaningless in the sunny, open landscape.

The group of figures is strikingly suggestive of Da Vinci, but the quiet, rural pasture in which the Virgin sits is Luini's own. In the distance is a thick clump of trees, finely drawn in stem and branch. At one side is a shepherd's hut with a flock of sheep grazing near. The child Jesus reaches from his mother's lap to play with the lamb which the little St. John has brought, a *motif* similar to Raphael's Madrid picture, and perhaps due, in both painters, to the example of Leonardo.

It is said by the learned that during the period of the Renaissance the love of nature received an immense impulse from the revival of the Latin poets, and that this impulse was felt most in the large cities. In the pictures noted, we have seen its effect in Florentine and Lombard art; that it was also felt in isolated places, we may see in some of Correggio's work at Parma, at about the same time. Two, at least, of his Madonna pictures are as famous for their beautiful landscapes as for the rare grace and charm of their figures. These are the kneeling Madonna, of the Uffizi, and "La Zingarella," at Naples. Both show a perfect adaptation of the surroundings to the spirit of the scene. In the first it is morning, and the gladness of Nature reflects the Mother's rapturous joy in her awakening babe. A brilliant light floods the figures in the foreground and melts across the green slopes into the hazy distance of the sea-bound horizon. In the second it is twilight, and a calm stillness broods over all, as under the feathery palms the Mother bends, watchful, over her little one's slumbers. Such were the revelations of Nature to the country-bred painter from the little town of Correggio.

Turning now to Venice for our last

examples, we find that the love of natural scenery was remarkably strong in this city of water and sky, where the very absence of verdure may have created a homesick longing for the green fields. It was Venetian art which originated that form of pastoral Madonna known as the Santa Conversazione. This is usually a long, narrow picture, showing a group of sacred personages, against a landscape setting, centering about the Madonna and child. The composition has none of the formality of the enthroned Madonna. An underlying unity of purpose and action binds all the figures together in natural and harmonious relations.

The acknowledged leader of this style of composition — the inventor indeed, according to many — was Palma Vecchio. It is curious that of a painter whose works are so widely admired, almost nothing is known. Even the traditions which once lent color to his life have been shattered by the ruthless hand of the modern investigator. The span of his life extended from 1480 to 1528. Thus he came at the beginning of the century made glorious by Titian, and contributed not a little in his own way to its glory.

It is supposed that he studied under Giovanni Bellini, and at one time was a friend and colleague of Lorenzo Lotto. A child of the mountains — for he was born in Serinalta — he never entirely lost the influence of his early surroundings.

To the last his figures are grave, vigorous, sometimes almost rude, partaking of the characteristics of the everlasting hills. Perhaps it was these traits which made the Santa Conversazione a favorite composition with him. He has an intense love of Nature in her most luxuriant mood.

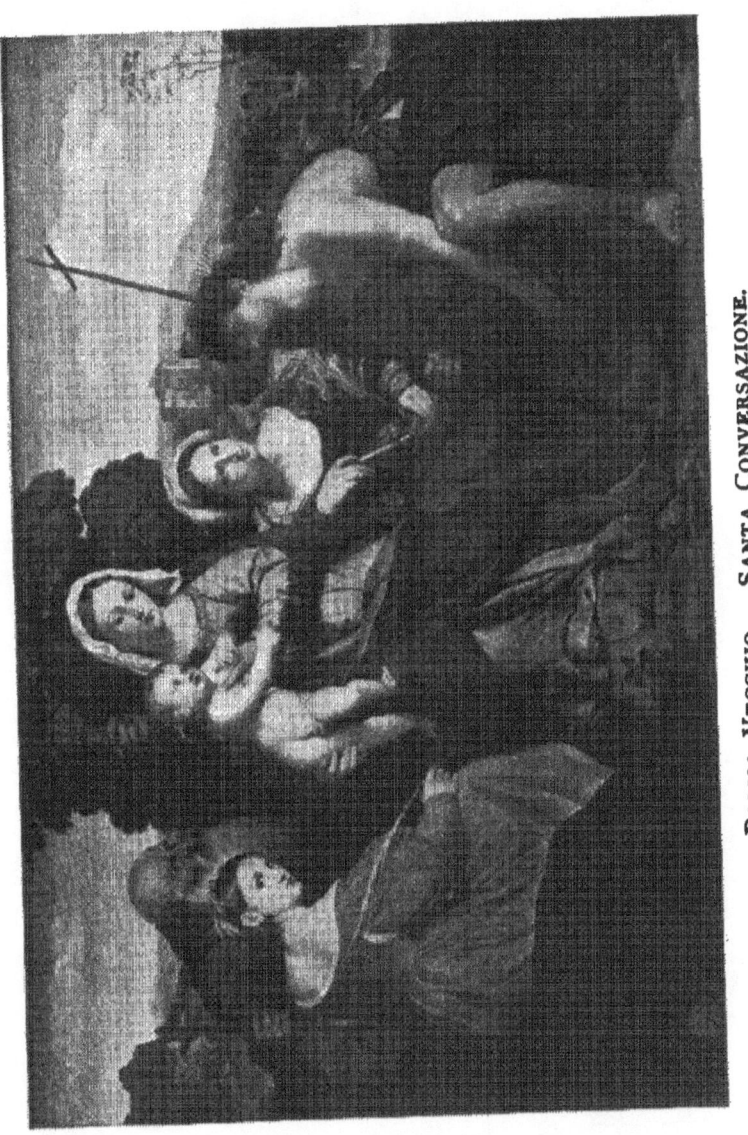

PALMA VECCHIO.—SANTA CONVERSAZIONE.

For a collection of Palma's pictures, we should choose at least four to represent his treatment of the Santa Conversazione: those at Naples, Dresden, Munich, and Vienna. The Naples picture is considered the most successful of Palma's large pictures of this kind, but it is not easy for the less critical observer to choose a favorite among the four. One general formula describes them all: a sunny landscape with hills clad in their greenest garb; a tree in the foreground, beneath which sits the Virgin, a comely, country-bred matron, who seems to have drawn her splendid vigor from the clear, bright air. On her lap she supports a sprightly little boy, who is the centre of attention.

In the simpler compositions the Madonna is at the left, and at the right kneel or sit two saints. One is a handsome young rustic, unkempt and roughly clad, sometimes figuring as St. John the Baptist, and sometimes as St. Roch. With him is contrasted a beautiful young female saint, usually St. Catherine. Where the composition includes other figures, the Virgin is in the centre, with the attendant personages symmetrically grouped on either side. In the Vienna picture the two additional figures at the left are the aged St. Celestin and a fine St. Barbara.

Of all schools of painting, the Venetian is the least translatable into black and white, so rich in colors is the palette which composed it. This is especially true of Palma, and to understand aright his Santa Conversazione, we must read into it the harmony of colors which it expresses, the chords of blue, red, brown, and green, the shimmering lights and brilliant atmosphere.

The subject of the Santa Conversazione should not be left without a brief reference to other Venetians, who added to the pop-

FILIPPINO LIPPI. — MADONNA IN A ROSE GARDEN.

ularity of this charming style of picture. Berenson mentions seven by Palma's pupil, Bonifazio Veronese, and one by his friend, Lorenzo Lotto. Cima, Cariani, Paris Bordone, and last, but not least, the great Titian,[1] lent their gifts to the subject, so that we have abundant evidence of the Venetian love of natural scenery.

It remains to consider one more form of the pastoral Madonna, that which represents the Virgin and child in "a garden inclosed," in allusion to the symbolism of Solomon's Song (4 : 12). The subject is found among the woodcuts of Albert Dürer, but I have never seen it in any German painting.

In Italian art there are two famous pictures of this class: by Francia, in the Munich Gallery, and by Filippino Lippi (or so attributed), in the Pitti, at Flor-

[1] See particularly Titian's works in the Louvre, of which the Vierge au Lapin is an especially charming pastoral.

ence. In both the *motif* is the same:
in the foreground, a square inclosure
surrounded by a rose-hedge, with a hilly
landscape in the distance; the Virgin
kneeling before her child in the centre.
Filippino Lippi's is one of those pictures whose beauty attracts crowds of
admirers to the canvas.. Copyists are
kept busy, repeating the composition for
eager purchasers, and it has made its
way all over the world. The circle of
graceful angels who, with the boy St.
John, join the mother in adoring the
Christ-child, is one of the chief attractions
of the picture.   It is a pretty conceit that
one of these angels showers rose leaves
upon the babe.

The pastoral Madonna is the sort of
picture which can never be outgrown.
The charm of nature is as perennial as
is the beauty of motherhood, and the two
are always in harmony.   Here, then, is a

proper subject for modern Madonna art, a field which has scarcely been opened by the artists of our own day. Such pastoral Madonnas as have been painted within recent years are all more or less artificial in conception. Compared with the idyllic charm of the sixteenth century pictures, they seem like pretty scenes in a well-mounted opera. We are looking for better things.

CHAPTER V.

SUBJECT so sacred as the Madonna was long held in too great reverence to permit of any common or realistic treatment. The pastoral setting brought the mother and her babe into somewhat closer and more human relations than had before been deemed possible; but art was slow to presume any further upon this familiarity. The Madonna as a domestic subject, represented in the interior of her home, was hesitatingly adopted, and has been so rarely treated, even down to our own times, as to form but a small group of pictures in the great body of art.

The Northern painters naturally led

SCHONGAUER. — HOLY FAMILY.

the way. Peculiarly home-loving in their tastes, their ideal woman is the *hausfrau*, and it was with them no lowering of the Madonna's dignity to represent her in this capacity. A picture in the style of Quentin Massys hangs in the Munich Gallery, and shows a Flemish bedroom of the fifteenth century. At the left stands the bed, and on the right burns the fire, with a kettle hanging over it. The Virgin sits alone with her babe at her breast.

More frequently a domestic scene of this sort includes other figures belonging to the Holy Family. A typical German example is the picture by Schongauer in the Belvedere Gallery at Vienna. The Virgin is seated in homely surroundings, intent upon a bunch of grapes which she holds in her hands, and which she has taken from a basket standing on the floor beside her. Long, waving hair falls over

her shoulders ; a snowy kerchief is folded
primly in the neck of her dress; she
is the impersonation of virgin modesty.
Her baby boy stands on her lap, nestling
against his mother; his eyes fixed on
the fruit, his eager little face glowing
with pleasure. Beyond are seen the cat-
tle, which Joseph is feeding. He pauses
at the door, a bundle of hay in his arms,
to look in with fond pride at his young
wife and her child.

Schongauer's work belongs to the latter
part of the fifteenth century, and there
was nothing similar to it in Italy at the
same period. It is true that Madonnas in
domestic settings have been attributed to
contemporaneous Italians, but they were
probably by some Flemish hand.

Giulio Romano, a pupil of Raphael,
was perhaps the first of the Italians to
give any domestic touch to the subject
of the Madonna and child. His Ma-

RAPHAEL. — MADONNA DELL' IMPANNATA.

donna della Catina of the Dresden Gallery is well known. It is so called from
the basin in which the Christ-child stands
while the little St. John pours in water
from a pitcher for the bath. Another
picture by the same artist shows the
Madonna seated with her child in the
interior of a bedchamber. This was one
of the "discoveries" of the late Senator
Giovanni Morelli, the critic, and is in a
private collection in Dresden.

To Giulio Romano also, according to
recent criticism, is due the domestic Madonna known as the "Impannata," and
usually attributed to Raphael. It is prob-
able that both artists had a hand in it,
the master in the arrangement of the
composition, the pupil in its execution.
A bed at one side is concealed by a green
curtain. In the rear is the cloth-covered
window which gives the picture its name.
Elizabeth and Mary Magdalene have

brought home the child, who springs to his mother's arms, smiling back brightly at his friends. One other Madonna from Raphael's brush (the Orleans) has an interior setting, but the domestic environment here is undoubtedly the work of some Flemish painter of later date.

By the seventeenth century, the Holy Family in a home environment can be found somewhat more often in various localities. By the French painter Mignard there is a well-known picture in the Louvre called La Vierge à la Grappe. By F. Barocci of Urbino there is an example in the National Gallery known as the Madonna del Gatto, in which the child holds a bird out of the reach of a cat. A similar *motif*, certainly not a pleasant one, is seen in Murillo's Holy Family of the Bird, in Madrid. By Salimbeni, in the Pitti, is a Holy Family in an interior, showing the boy Jesus and his cousin St. John playing with puppies.

Rembrandt's domestic Madonna pictures, equally homely as to environment, are by no means scenes of hilarity, but rather of frugal contentment.   Two similar works bear the title of Le Ménage du Menuisier — the Carpenter's Home.   In both, the scene is the interior of a common room devoted to work and household purposes.   Joseph is seen in the rear at his bench, while the central figures are the mother and child.

In the Louvre picture, the Virgin's mother is present, caressing her grandchild, who is held at his mother's breast. The composition at St. Petersburg (Hermitage Gallery) is simpler, and shows the Virgin contemplating her babe as he lies asleep in the cradle.   Another well-known picture by Rembrandt is in the Munich Gallery, where again we have signs of the carpenter's toil, but where the laborer has stopped for a moment to peep at the babe, who has gone off to dreamland at his mother's breast and now sleeps sweetly in her lap. Let those who think such pictures too homely for a sacred theme compare them with the simplicity of the Gospels.

PART II.

MADONNAS CLASSED ACCORDING TO THEIR SIGNIFICANCE AS TYPES OF MOTHERHOOD.

CHAPTER VI.

THE MADONNA OF LOVE.

(THE MATER AMABILIS.)

UNDOUBTEDLY the most popular of all Madonna subjects — certainly the most easily understood — is the Mater Amabilis. The mother's mood may be read at a glance: she is showing in one of a thousand tender ways her motherly affection for her child. She clasps him in her arms, holding him to her breast, pressing her face to his, kissing him, caressing him, or playing with him. Love is written in every line of her face; love is the key-note of the picture.

The style of composition best adapted to such a theme is manifestly the simplest.

The more formal types of the enthroned and glorified Madonnas are the least suitable for the display of maternal affection, while the portrait Madonna, and the Madonna in landscape or domestic scenes, are readily conceived as the Mater Amabilis. Nevertheless, these distinctions have not by any means been rigidly regarded in art. This is manifest in some of the illustrations in Part I., as the Enthroned Madonna, by Quentin Massys, where the mother kisses her child, and Angelico's Madonna in Glory, where she holds him to her cheek.

Gathering our examples from so many methods of composition, we are in the midst of a multitude of pictures which no man can number, and which set forth every conceivable phase of motherliness.

Let us make Raphael our starting-point. From the same master whose influence led him to the study of external nature, he

,learned also the study of human nature.
To the interpretation of mother-love he
brought all the fresh ardor of youth, and
a sunny temperament which saw only joy
in the face of Nature. One after another
of the series of his Florentine pictures
gives us a new glimpse of the loving relation between mother and child.

The Belle Jardinière gazes into her
boy's face in fond absorption. The Tempi
Madonna holds him to her heart, pressing
her lips to his soft cheek. In the Orleans
and Colonna pictures she smiles indul-
gently into his eyes as he lies across her
lap, plucking at the bosom of her dress.
Other pictures show the two eagerly reading together from the Book of Wisdom
(The Conestabile and Ansidei Madonnas).

The painter's later work evinces a
growing maturity of thought. In the
Holy Family of Francis I., how strong
and tender is the mother's attitude, as

she stoops to lift her child from his cradle;
in the Chair Madonna, how protecting is
the capacious embrace with which she
gathers him to herself in brooding love.
No technical artistic education is necessary for the appreciation of such pictures.
All who have known a mother's love look
and understand, and look again and are
satisfied.

Correggio touches the heart in much
the same way; he, too, saw the world
through rose-colored glasses. His interpretation of life is full of buoyant en-
joyment. Beside the tranquil joy of
Raphael's ideals, his figures express a
tumultuous gladness, an overflowing gay-
ety. This is the more curious because
of the singular melancholy which is attributed to him. The outer circumstances
of his life moved in a quiet groove which
was almost humdrum. He passed his
days in comparative obscurity at Parma,

far from the great art influences of his
time.   But isolation seemed the better
to develop his rare individuality.   He
was the architect of his own fortunes,
and wrought out independently a style
peculiar to himself.   His most famous
Madonna pictures are large compositions,
crowded with figures of extravagant atti-
tudes and expression.   The fame of these
more pretentious works rests not so much
upon their inner significance as upon
their splendid technique.   They are un-
surpassed for masterly handling of color,
and for triumphs of chiaroscuro.

There are better qualities of sentiment
in the smaller pictures, where the mother
is alone with her child.   It is here that
we find something worthy to compare
with Raphael.   There are several of these,
produced in rapid succession during the
period when the artist was engaged upon
the frescoes of S. Giovanni (Parma), and

soon after marriage had opened his heart
to sweet, domestic influences.

The first was the Uffizi picture, so
widely known and loved. The mother
has gathered up her mantle so that it
covers her head and drops at one side
on a step, forming a soft, blue cushion
for the babe. Here the little darling lies,
looking up into his mother's face. Kneeling on the step below, she bends over
him, with her hands playfully outstretched,
in a transport of maternal affection.

Following this came the picture now in
the National Gallery, called the Madonna
della Cesta, from the basket that lies on
the ground. It is a domestic scene in
the outer air: the mother is dressing
her babe, and smilingly arrests his hand,
which, on a sudden impulse, he has
stretched towards some coveted object.
The same face is almost exactly repeated
in the Madonna of the Hermitage Gallery

(St. Petersburg), who offers her breast to her boy, at that moment turning about to receive some fruit presented by a child angel. There are two duplicates of this picture in other galleries.

The Zingarella (the Gypsy) is so called from the gypsy turban worn by the Madonna. The mother, supposed to be painted from the artist's wife, sits with the child asleep on her lap. With motherly tenderness she bends so closely over him that her forehead touches his little head. It is unfortunate that this beautiful work is not better known. It is in the Naples Gallery.

A comparison of these pictures discloses a remarkable variety in action and grouping. On the other hand, the Madonnas are quite similar in general type. With the exception of the Zingarella, who is the most motherly, they are all in a playful mood. The same playfulness, but of a more sweet and motherly kind, lights the face of the Madonna della Scala. The composition is somewhat in the portrait style, showing the mother in half length, seated under a sort of canopy. The babe clings closely to her neck, turning about at the spectator with a glance half shy and half mischievous. His coyness awakens a smile of tender amusement in the gentle, young face above him.

The picture has an interesting history. It was originally painted in fresco over the eastern gate of Parma, where Vasari saw and admired it. In after years, the wall which it decorated was incorporated into a small new church, of which it formed the rear wall. To accommodate the high level of the Madonna, the building was somewhat elevated, and, being entered by a flight of steps, was known as S. Maria della Scala (of the staircase). The name attached itself to the picture

CORREGGIO. — MADONNA DELLA SCALA.

even after the church was destroyed (in 1812), and the fresco removed to the town gallery. The marks of defacement which it bears are due to the votive offerings which were formerly fastened upon it, — among them, a silver crown worn by the Madonna as late as the eighteenth century. Though such scars injure its artistic beauty, they add not a little to the romantic interest which invests it.

Beside such names as Raphael and Correggio, history furnishes but one other worthy of comparison for the portrayal of the Mater Amabilis — it is Titian. His Madonna is by no means uniformly motherly. There are times when we look in vain for any softening of her aristocratic features; when her stately dignity seems quite incompatible with demonstrativeness.[1] But when love melts her heart

[1] See the Madonna of the Cherries in the Belvedere at Vienna, and the Madonna and Saints in the Dresden Gallery.

how gracious is her unbending, how winning her smile! Once she goes so far as
to play in the fields with her little boy,
quieting a rabbit with one hand for him
to admire. (La Vierge au Lapin, Louvre.)
In other pictures she holds him lying
across her lap, smiling thoughtfully upon
him. Such an one is the Madonna with
Sts. Ulfo and Brigida, in the Madrid Gallery. The child is taking the flowers St.
Brigida offers him, and his mother looks
down with the pleased expression of fond
pride. Again, when her babe holds his
two little hands full of the roses his cousin
St. John has brought him, she smiles
gently at the eagerness of the two children. (Uffizi Gallery.)

Another similar composition reveals a
still sweeter intimacy between mother and
son. The babe stretches out his hand
coaxingly towards his mother's breast, but
she draws her veil about her, gently deny-

TITIAN. — MADONNA AND SAINTS. (DETAIL.)

ing his appeal. A more beautiful mother, or a more bewitching babe, it were hard to find. Three fine half-length figures of saints complete this composition, each of great interest and individuality, but not necessary to the unity of action — the Madonna alone making a complete picture. There are two copies of this work, one in the Belvedere at Vienna, and one in the Louvre at Paris.

The *motif* of this picture is not unique in art, as will have been remarked in passing. The first duty of maternity, and one of its purest joys, is to sustain the new-born life at the mother's breast. A coarse interpretation of the subject desecrates a holy shrine, while a delicate rendering, such as Raphael's or Titian's, invests it with a new beauty. Other pictures of this class should be mentioned in the same connection. There is one in the Hermitage Gallery at St. Petersburg, attributed by late critics to the little-known painter, Bernardino de' Conti. The Madonna's face, her hair drawn smoothly over her temples, has a beautiful matronliness. Still another is the Madonna of the Green Cushion, by Solario, in the Louvre. Here the babe lies on a cushion before his mother, who bends over him ecstatically, her fair young face aglow with maternal love as she sees his contentment.

We have noticed that in one of Corregio's pictures the babe lies asleep on his mother's lap. It is interesting to trace this pretty *motif* through other works of art. No phase of motherhood is more touching than the watchful care which guards the child while he sleeps; nor is infancy ever more appealing than in peaceful and innocent slumber. Mrs. Browning understood this well, when she wrote her beautiful poem interpreting the thoughts of "the Virgin Mary to the Child Jesus." Hopes and fears, joy and pity, are alternately stirred in the heart of the watcher, as she bends over the tiny face, scanning every change that flits across it. Each verse suggests a subject for a picture.

We should naturally expect that Raphael would not overlook so beautiful a theme as the mother watching her sleeping child. Nor are we disappointed. The Madonna of the Diadem, in the Louvre, belongs to this class of pictures. Like the pastoral Madonnas of the Florentine period, it includes the figure of the little St. John, to whom, in this instance, the proud mother is showing her babe, daintily lifting the veil which covers his face.

The seventeenth century produced many pictures of this class; among them, a beautiful work by Guido Reni, in Rome, deserves mention, being executed with greater care than was usual with him. Sassoferrato and Carlo Dolce frequently painted the subject. Their Madonnas often seem affected, not to say sentimental, after the simpler and nobler types of the earlier period. But nowhere is their peculiar sweetness more appropriate than beside a sleeping babe. The Corsini picture by Carlo Dolce is an exquisite nursery scene. Its popularity depends more, perhaps, upon the babe than the mother. Like Lady Isobel's child in another poem of motherhood by Mrs. Browning, he sleeps —

> "Fast, warm, as if its mother's smile,
> Laden with love's dewy weight,
> And red as rose of Harpocrate,
> Dropt upon its eyelids, pressed
> Lashes to cheek in a sealèd rest."

In Northern Madonna art, the Mater Amabilis is the preëminent subject.

This fact is due partly to the German theological tendency to subordinate the mother to her divine Son, but more especially to the characteristic domesticity of Teutonic peoples. From Van Eyck and Schongauer, through Dürer and Holbein, down to Rembrandt and Rubens, we trace this strongly marked predilection in every style of composition, regardless of proprieties. Van Eyck does not hesitate to occupy his richly dressed enthroned Madonna at Frankfort with giving her breast to her babe, and Dürer portrays the same maternal duties in the Virgin on the Crescent Moon. Holbein's Meyer Madonna, splendid with her jewelled crown, is not less motherly than Schongauer's young Virgin sitting in a rude stable.

Rembrandt in humble Dutch interiors, Rubens in numerous Holy Families modelled upon the Flemish life about him always conceive of the Virgin Mother as delighting in her maternal cares. As has been said of Dürer's Madonna, — and the description applies equally well to many others in the North,— "She suckles her son with a calm feeling of happiness; she gazes upon him with admiration as he lies upon her lap; she caresses him and presses him to her bosom without a thought whether it is becoming to her, or whether she is being admired."

This entire absence of posing on the part of the German Virgin is one of the most admirable elements in this art. This characteristic is perfectly illustrated in Dürer's portrait Madonna of the Belvedere Gallery, at Vienna. This is an excellent specimen of the master, who, alone of the Germans, is considered the peer of his great Italian contemporaries. Frankly admired both by Titian and Raphael, he has in common with them

DÜRER. — MADONNA AND CHILD.

the supreme gift of seeing and repro-
ducing natural human affections. His
work, however, is as thoroughly German
as theirs is Italian. The Madonna of
this picture has the round, maidenly face
of the typical German ideal. A trans-
parent veil droops over the flowing hair,
covered by a blue drapery above. The
mother holds her child high in her
arms, bending her face over him. The
babe is a beautiful little fellow, full of
vivacity. He holds up a pear gleefully, to
meet his mother's smile. The picture is
painted with great delicacy of finish.

The Mater Amabilis is the subject
par excellence of modern Madonna art.
Carrying on its surface so much beauty
and significance, it is naturally attractive
to all figure painters. While other Madonna subjects are too often beyond the
comprehension of either the artist or his
patron, this falls within the range of both.

The shop windows are full of pretty pictures of this kind, in all styles of treatment.

There are the portrait Madonnas by Gabriel Max, already mentioned, and pastoral Madonnas by Bouguereau, by Carl Müller, by N. Barabino, and by Dagnan-Bouveret. Others carry the subject into the more formal compositions of the enthroned and enskied Madonnas, being, as we have seen, not without illustrious predecessors among the old masters. Of these we have Guay's Mater Amabilis, where the mother leans from her throne to support her child, playing on the step below with his cousin, St. John; and Mary L. Macomber's picture, where the enthroned Madonna folds her babe in her protecting arms, as if to shield him from impending evil.

By Bodenhausen we have the extremely popular Mater Amabilis in Gloria, where

BODENHAUSEN. — MADONNA AND CHILD.

a girlish young mother, her long hair streaming about her, stands in upper air, poised above the great ball of the earth, holding her sweet babe to her heart. .

Pictures like these constantly reiterate the story of a mother's love — an old, old story, which begins again with every new birth.

CHAPTER VII.

THE MADONNA IN ADORATION.

(THE MADRE PIA.)

HE first tender joys of a mother's love are strangely mingled with awe. Her babe is a precious gift of God, which she receives into trembling hands. A new sense of responsibility presses upon her with almost overwhelming force. Hers is the highest honor given unto woman; she accepts it with solemn joy, deeming herself all too unworthy.

This spirit of humility has been idealized in art, in the form of Madonna known as the Madre Pia. It represents the Virgin Mary adoring her son. Sometimes she kneels before him, sometimes she sits with clasped hands, holding him in her lap. Whatever the variation in attitude, the thought is the same: it is an expression of that higher, finer aspect of motherhood which regards infancy as an object not only of love, but of reverent humility. It is a recognition of the great mystery of life which invests even the helpless babe with a dignity commanding respect.

A picture with so serious an intention can never be widely understood. The meaning is too subtile for the casual observer. An outgrowth of mediæval pietism, it was superseded by more popular subjects, and has never since been revived. The subject had its origin as an idealized nativity, set in pastoral surroundings which suggest the Bethlehem manger. Theologically it represented the Virgin as the first worshipper of her divine Son. But though the sacred mystery of Mary's experience sets her forever apart as "blessed among women," she is the type of true motherhood in all generations.

The Madonna in Adoration is, properly speaking, a fifteenth century subject. It belongs primarily to that most mystic of all schools of art, the Umbrian, centering in the town of Perugia. Nowhere else was painting so distinctly an adjunct of religious services, chiefly designed to aid the worshipper in prayer and contemplation.

As an exponent of the typical qualities of the Perugian school stands the artist who is known by its name, Perugino. His favorite subject is the Madre Pia, and his best picture of the kind is the Madonna of the National Gallery. Having once seen her here, the traveller recognizes her again and again in other galleries, in the many replicas of this charming composition. The Madonna kneels in the fore-

ground, adoring with folded hands the
child, who is supported in a sitting pos-
ture on the ground, by a guardian angel.
The Virgin's face is full of fervent and
exalted emotion.

Perugino had no direct imitator of his
Madre Pia, but his Bolognese admirer
Francia treated the subject in a way that
readily suggests the source of his inspiration. His Madonna of the Rose Garden
in Munich instantly recalls Perugino. The
artist has, however, chosen a novel *motif*
in representing the moment when the
Virgin is just sinking on her knees, as if
overcome by emotion.

Between the Umbrian school and the
Florentine, a reciprocal influence was exerted. If the latter taught the former
many secrets of composition and technical execution, the Umbrians in turn im-
parted something of their mysticism to
their more matter-of-fact neighbors. While

the Umbrian school of the fifteenth century was occupied with the Madre Pia,
Florence also was devoted to the same
subject. Sculpture led the race, and in
the front ranks was Luca della Robbia,
founder of the school which bears his
family name.

Beginning as a worker in marble, his
inventive genius presently wrought out
a style of sculpture peculiarly his own.
This was the enamelled terra-cotta bas-
relief showing pure white figures against
a background of pale blue. They were
made chiefly in circular medallions, lu-
nettes, and tabernacles, and were scattered
throughout the churches and homes of
Tuscany.

Associated with Luca in his work was
his nephew Andrea, who, in turn, had
three sculptor sons, Giovanni, Girolamo,
and Luca II. So great was the demand
for their ware that the Della Robbia

studios became a veritable manufactory from which hundreds of pieces went forth. Of these, a goodly number represent the Madonna in Adoration. While it is difficult to trace every one of these with absolute correctness to its individual author, the majority seem to be by Andrea, who, as it would appear, had a special fondness for the subject. It must be acknowledged that the nephew is inferior to his uncle in his ideal of the Virgin, less original than Luca in his conceptions, and less noble in his results. His work, notwithstanding, has many charming qualities, which are specially appropriate to the character of the particular subject under consideration. There is, indeed, a peculiar value in low relief, for purposes of idealization. It has an effect of spiritualizing the material, and giving the figures an ethereal appearance. Andrea profited by this advantage, and, in addition, showed great delicacy of judgment in subduing curves and retaining simplicity in his lines.

We may see all this in the popular tabernacle which he designed, and of which there are at least five, and probably more, copies. The Madonna kneels prayerfully before her babe, who lies on the ground by some lily stalks. In the sky above are two cherubim and hands holding a crown. There is a girlish grace in the kneeling figure, and a rare sweetness in the face, entirely free from sentimentality. A severe simplicity of drapery, and the absence of all unnecessary accessories, are points of excellence worth noting. The composition was sometimes varied by the introduction of different figures in the sky, other cherubim, or the head of the Almighty, with the Dove. Only second in popularity to this was Andrea's circular medallion of the Na-

ANDREA DELLA ROBBIA. — MADONNA IN ADORATION.

tivity, with the Virgin and St. John in adoration. There are two copies of this in the Florentine Academy, one in the Louvre, and one in Berlin. The effect of crowding so many figures into a small compass is not so pleasing as the classical simplicity of the former composition.

Contemporary with the Della Robbias was another Florentine family of artists equally numerous. Of the five Rossellini, Antonio is of greatest interest to us, as a sculptor who had some qualities in common with the famous porcelain workers. Like them, he had a special gift for the Madonna in Adoration. We can see this subject in his best style of treatment, in the beautiful Nativity in San Miniato, "which may be regarded as one of the most charming productions of the best period of Tuscan art." [1] The

[1] C. C. Perkins, in Tuscan Sculptors.

tourist will consider it a rich reward for his climb to the quaint old church on the ramparts overhanging the Arno. If perchance his wanderings lead him, on another occasion, to the hill rising on the opposite side, he will find, in the Cathedral of Fiesole, a fitting companion in the altar-piece by Mino da Fiesole. This is a decidedly unique rendering of the Madre Pia. The Virgin kneels in a niche, facing the spectator, adoring the Christ-child, who sits on the steps below her, turning to the little Baptist, who kneels at one side on a still lower step.

Passing from the sculpture of Florence to its painting, it is fitting that we mention first of all the friend and fellow-pupil of the Umbrian Perugino, Lorenzo di Credi. The two had much in common. Trained together in the workshop of the sculptor Verrocchio, in those days of intense religious stress, they both became

LORENZO DI CREDI. — NATIVITY.

followers of the prophet-prior of San
Marco, Savonarola. Their religious earnestness naturally found expression in the
beautiful subject of the Madre Pia. The
Florentine artist, though not less devout
than his friend, introduces into his work
an element of joy, characteristic of his
surroundings, and more attractive than
the somewhat melancholy types of Um-
bria. His Adoration, in the Uffizi, is
an admirable example of his best work.
Following the fashion made popular by
the Della Robbias, the artist chose for
his composition the round picture, or
tondo. By this elimination of unnecessary corners, the attention centres in the
beautiful figure of the Virgin, which
occupies a large portion of the circle.
In exquisite keeping with the modest
loveliness of her face, a delicate, trans-
parent veil is knotted over her smooth
hair, and falls over the round curves of

her neck. In expression and attitude she is the perfect impersonation of the spirit of humility, joyfully submissive to her high calling, reverently acknowledging her unworthiness.

This picture may be taken as a typical example of the subject in Florentine painting. Lorenzo himself repeated the composition many times, and numerous other works could be mentioned, strikingly similar in treatment, by Ghirlandajo, in the Florence Academy; by Signorelli, in the National Gallery; by Albertinelli, in the Pitti; by Filippo Lippi, in the Berlin Gallery; by Filippino Lippi, in the Pitti; and so on through the list.

In many cases the subject seems to have been chosen, not so much from any devotional spirit on the part of the painter, as from force of imitation of the prevailing Florentine fashion. This is especially true in the case of Filippo Lippi, who does not bear the best of reputations. Although a brother in the Carmelite monastery, his love of worldly pleasures often led him astray, if we are to believe the gossip of the old annalists. We may allow much for the exaggerations of scandal, but still be forced to admit that his candid realism is plain evidence of a closer study of nature than of theology.

Browning has given us a fine analysis of his character in the poem bearing his name, " Fra Lippo Lippi." The artist monk, caught in the streets of the city on his return from some midnight revel, explains his constant quarrel with the rules of art laid down by ecclesiastical authorities. They insist that his business is "to the souls of men," and that it is "quite from the mark of painting" to make "faces, arms, legs, and bodies like the true." On his part, he claims that it will not help the interpretation of soul, by painting body ill. An intense lover of every beautiful line and color in God's world, he believes that these things are given us to be thankful for, not to pass over or despise. Obliged to devote himself to a class of subjects with which he had little sympathy, he compromised with his critics by adopting the traditional forms of composition, and treating them after the manner of *genre* painters, in types drawn from the ordinary life about him. The kneeling Madre Pia he painted three times: two of the pictures are in the Florence Academy, and the third and best is in the Berlin Gallery.

In the Madonna of the Uffizi, he broke away somewhat from tradition, and rendered quite a new version of the subject. The Virgin is seated with folded hands, adoring her child, who is held up before her by two boy angels. His type of child-

FILIPPO LIPPI. — MADONNA IN ADORATION.

hood is by no means pretty, though altogether natural. The Virgin cannot be
called either intellectual or spiritual, but
" where," as a noted critic has asked, " can
we find a face more winsome and appealing?" Certainly she is a lovely woman,
and

" If you get simple beauty and naught else,
    That's somewhat: and you'll find the soul you
        have missed
    Within yourself, when you return him thanks."

The idea of the seated Madre Pia, comparatively rare in Florentine art, is quite
frequent in northern Italy. Sometimes
the setting is a landscape, in the foreground of which the Madonna sits adoring the babe lying on her lap. Examples are by Basaiti (Paduan), in the
National Gallery, and by a painter of
Titian's school, in Berlin. Much more
common is the enthroned Madonna in

Adoration, and for this we may turn to the pictures of the Vivarini, Bartolommeo and Luigi, or Alvise. These men were of Muranese origin, and in the very beginning of Venetian art - history were at the head of their profession, until finally eclipsed by the rival family of the Bellini. Among their works, we find by each one at least three pictures of the type described. As the most worthy of description, we may select the altar-piece by Luigi, in the Church of the Redentore. As it is one of the most popular Madonnas in Venice, no collection is complete without it. A green curtain forms the background, against which the plain marble throne-chair is brought into relief. The Virgin sits wrapt in her own thoughts, an impersonation of tranquil dignity. A heavy wimple falls low over her forehead, entirely concealing her hair, and with its severe simplicity accentuating the chaste

LUIGI VIVARINI. — MADONNA AND CHILD.

beauty of her face. Two fascinating little cherubs sit on a parapet in front, playing on lutes; and, lulled by their gentle music, the sweet babe sleeps on, serenely unconscious of it all.

Before such pictures as this, gleaming in the dim light of quiet chapels, many a heart, before unbelieving, may learn a new reverence for the mysterious sanctity of motherhood.

CHAPTER VIII.

THE MADONNA AS WITNESS.

N proportion to a mother's ideals and ambitions for her child does her love take on a higher and purer aspect. The noblest mother is the most unselfish; she regards her child as a sacred charge, only temporarily committed to her keeping. Her care is to nurture and train him for his part in life; this is the object of her constant endeavor. Thus she comes to look upon him as hers and yet not hers. In one sense he is her very own; in another, he belongs to the universal life which he is to serve. There is no conflict between the two ideas; they are the obverse sides of one great truth. Both must be recognized for a complete understanding of life. What is true of all motherhood finds a supreme illustration in the character of the Virgin Mary. She understood from the first that her son had a great mission to fulfil, that his work had somewhat to do with a mighty kingdom. Never for a moment did she lose sight of these things as she " pondered them in her heart." Her highest joy was to present him to the world for the fulfilment of his calling.

As a subject of art, this phase of the Madonna's character requires a mode of treatment quite unlike that of the Mater Amabilis or the Madre Pia. The attitude and expression of the Virgin are appropriate to her office as the Christ-bearer. Both mother and child, no longer absorbed in each other, direct their glance towards the people to whom he is given for a witness. (Isaiah 55: 4.) These may be the spectators looking at the picture, or the saints and votaries filling the composition. The mother's lap is the throne for the child, from which, standing or sitting, he gives his royal blessing.

It will be readily understood that so lofty a theme can not be common in art. In our own day, it has, with the Madre Pia, passed almost entirely out of the range of art subjects; modern painters do not try such heights. Franz Defregger is alone in having made an honest and earnest effort, not without success, to express his conception of the theme. To his Enthroned Madonna at Dölsach, and his less well-known Madonna in Glory, let us pay this passing word of honor.

To approach our subject in the most systematic way, we will go back to the beginnings of Madonna art. Mrs. Jameson tells us that the group of Virgin and Son was, in its first intention, a

theological symbol, and not a *representation.* It was a device set up in the ortho-
dox churches as a definite formalization
of a creed. The first Madonnas showed
none of the aspects of ordinary motherhood in attitude, gesture, or expression.
The theological element in the picture
was the first consideration. We may
take as a representative case the Virgin
Nike-peja (of Victory), supposed to be
the same which Eudocia, wife of the
Emperor Theodosius II., discovered in
her travels in Palestine, and sent to
Constantinople, whence it was finally
brought to St. Mark's, Venice. The
Virgin — a half-length figure — holds the
child in front of her, like a doll, as if
exhibiting him to the gaze of the wor-
shippers before the altar over which the
picture hung. Both faces look directly
out at the spectator, with grave and stiff
solemnity.

The progress of painting, and the growing love of beauty, at length wrought a change. The time came when art saw the possibility of uniting, with the religious conception of previous centuries, a more natural ideal of motherhood. Thus, while the Madonna continues to be preëminently a witness of her son's greatness, it is not at the sacrifice of motherly tenderness.   •

In Venetian art-history, Giovanni Bellini stands at the period when the old was just merging into the new. We have already seen how greatly he and his contemporaries differed from the painters of a later time. Taking advantage of all the progressive methods of the day, they did not relinquish the religious spirit of their predecessors, hence their work embodies the best elements of the old and new. As we examine the Bellini Madonnas, one after another, we can not fail to notice how delicately they interpret the relation of the mother to her child.

Loving and gracious as she is, she is not the Mater Amabilis: she is too preoccupied, though not too cold for caresses. Neither is she the Madre Pia, though by no means lacking in humility. Her thoughts are of the future, rather than of the present. True to a mother's instinct, she encircles her child with a protecting arm, but her face is turned, not to his, but to the world. Both are looking steadfastly forward to the great work before them. Their eyes have the far-seeing look of those absorbed in noble dreams. Their faces are full of sweet earnestness, not of the ascetic sort, but joyful, with a calm, tranquil gladness.

This description applies almost equally well to a half-dozen or more of Bellini's Madonnas, in various styles of composition. For the sake of definiteness, we may specify the Madonna between St. Paul and St. George in the Venice Academy. The Virgin is in half-length, against a scarlet curtain, supporting the child, who stands on the coping of a balcony. In technical qualities alone, the picture is a notable one for precision of drawing, breadth of light and shade, and brilliant color. In Christian sentiment it is among the rare treasures of Italian art. The National Gallery and the Brera contain others which are very similar in style and conception.

The three enthroned Madonnas which have already been noticed are not less remarkable for religious significance. There is a peculiar freshness and vivacity in the San Giobbe picture. Both Virgin and child are alert and eager, welcoming the future with smiling and youthful enthusiasm. The Frari Ma-

GIOVANNI BELLINI. — MADONNA BETWEEN ST. GEORGE AND
ST. PAUL. (DETAIL.)

donna is of a more subdued type, but is not less true to her ideal. The Virgin of San Zaccaria is more thoughtful and reflective, but she holds her child up bravely, that he may give his blessing to mankind.

It will have been noticed that the throne is an especially appropriate setting for the Madonna as Witness. It is one of the functions of royalty that the queen should show the prince to his people. We therefore turn naturally to this class of pictures for examples. To those of Bellini just cited we may add, from the others mentioned in the second chapter, the Madonnas by Cima, by Palma, and by Montagna in Venetian Art; and by Luini and by Botticelli in the Lombard and Florentine schools respectively. Luini's picture is one which readily touches the heart. The Virgin unites the sweetness of fresh, young motherhood with womanly dignity of character. Her smile has nothing of mystery in it; it is simply sweet and winning. The Christ-child is a lovely boy, steadying himself against his mother's breast, and yet with an air of self-reliance. The two understand each other well.

One could hardly imagine two more dissimilar spirits than Luini and Botticelli. To Luini's Virgin, the consciousness of her son's greatness is a proud honor, accepted seriously, but gladly. To Botticelli, on the other hand, it brings a profound melancholy. This is so marked that at first sight almost every one is repelled by Botticelli, and yields only after long familiarity to the mysterious fascination of the sad-eyed Madonna, who holds her babe almost listlessly, as her head droops with the weight of her sorrow. Her expression is the same whatever her

LUINI. — MADONNA WITH ST. BARBARA AND ST. ANTHONY.

attitude, when she presses her babe to her bosom as the Mater Amabilis (in the Borghese Gallery at Rome, in the Dresden Gallery, and Louvre), or when, as witness to her son's destiny, she holds him forth to be seen of men. It is in this last capacity that her mood is most intelligible. She seems oppressed rather than humbled by her honors; reluctant, rather than glad to assume them; yet, with proud dignity, determined to do her part, though her heart break in the doing. Her nature is too deep to accept the joy without counting the cost, and her vision looks beyond Bethlehem to Calvary. This is well illustrated in the picture of the Berlin Gallery.[1] The queen

[1] The Berlin Gallery contains two Enthroned Madonnas attributed to Botticelli. The description here, and on page 40 makes it clear that the reference is to the picture numbered 102. This does not appear in Berenson's list of Botticelli's works, but is treated as authentic by Crowe and Cavalcaselle.

mother rises with the prince to receive the homage of humanity. The boy, old beyond his years, gravely raises his right hand to bless his people, the other still clinging, with infantile grace, to the dress of his mother. Lovely, rose-crowned angels hold court on either side, bearing lighted tapers in jars of roses.

The Madonna of the Pomegranate is another work by Botticelli which belongs in this class of pictures. It is a *tondo* in the Uffizi, showing the figures in half length. The Virgin, encircled by angels, holds the child half reclining on her lap. Her face is inexpressibly sad, and the child shares her mood, as he raises his little hand to bless the spectator. Two angels bear the Virgin's flowers, roses and lilies; two others hold books. They bend towards the queen as the petals of a rose bend towards the centre, with the serious grace peculiar to Botticelli.

BOTTICELLI. — MADONNA OF THE POMEGRANATE.

In connection with the peculiar type of melancholy exhibited on the face of Botticelli's Madonna, it will be of interest to refer to the work of Francia. The two artists were, in some points, kindred spirits; both felt the burden of life's mystery and sorrow. Francia, as we have seen, imbibed from the works of Perugino something of the spirit of mysticism common to the Umbrian school. But while there is a certain resemblance between his Madonna and Perugino's, the former has less of sentimentality than the latter, and more real melancholy. Like Botticelli's Virgin, she acts her part half-heartedly, as if the sword had already begun to pierce her heart. Francia's favorite Madonna subjects were of the higher order, the Madre Pia and the Madonna as Witness. In treating the latter, his Christ-child is always in keeping with the mother, a grave little fellow who gives the blessing with almost touching dignity. Enthroned Madonnas illustrating the theme are those of the Hermitage at St. Petersburg, of the Belvedere at Vienna, and the famous Bentivoglio Madonna in S. Jacopo Maggiore at Bologna. The last-named is one of the works which enable us to understand Raphael's high praise of the Bolognese master. It is a noble composition, full of strong religious feeling.

It is a long leap from the fifteenth to the seventeenth centuries, taking us from a period of genuine religious fervor in art, into an age of artificial imitation. In the midst of the decadence of old ideals and the birth of art methods entirely new, arose one who seemed to be the reincarnation of the old spirit in a form peculiar to his age and race. This was Murillo, the peasant-painter of Spain, than whom was never artist more pious, not even excepting the angelic brother of San Marco.

MURILLO. — MADONNA AND CHILD.

He alone in the seventeenth century kept
alive the pure flame of religious fervor,
which had burned within the devout
Italians of the early school.   Through all
his pictures of the Virgin and child we
can see that the Madonna as the Christ-
bearer is the ideal he always has in view.
He falls short of it, not through any lack
of earnestness, but because his type of
womanhood is incapable of expressing such
lofty idealism.   His virgins are modelled
upon the simple Andalusian maidens,
sweet, timid, dark-eyed creatures.   Their
faces glow with gentle affection as they
look wistfully out of the picture, or raise
their eyes to heaven, as if dimly discern-
ing the heights which they have never
reached.

The Pitti Madonna is one of this sweet
company, and perhaps the loveliest of
them all.   Both she and her beautiful boy
are full of gentle earnestness, and if they

are too simple-minded to realize what is in store for them, they are none the less ready to do the Father's will.

One more picture remains for us to consider as an illustration of the Madonna as Witness. Had we mentioned it first, nothing further could have been said on the subject. The Sistine Madonna is the greatest ever produced, from every point of view. We have already noted the superiority of its artistic composition over all other enskied Madonnas, and are the more ready to appreciate its higher merits; for its strongest hold upon our admiration is in its moral and religious significance. Its theme is the transfiguration of loving and consecrated motherhood. Mother and child, united in love, move towards the glorious consummation of the heavenly kingdom.

It has been said that Raphael made no preparatory studies for this Madonna,

RAPHAEL. — SISTINE MADONNA.

but, in a larger sense, he spent his life in preparation for it. He had begun by imitating the mystic sweetness of Perugino's types, drawn by an intuitive delicacy of perception to this spiritual idealism, while yet too inexperienced to express any originality. Then, by an inevitable reaction, he threw himself into the creation of a purely naturalistic Madonna, and carried the Mater Amabilis to its utmost perfection. Having mastered all the secrets of woman's beauty, he returned once more to the higher realm of idealism to send forth his matured conception of the Madonna as the Christ-bearer.

The Sistine Madonna is above all words of praise; all extravagance of expression is silenced before her simplicity. Hers is the beauty of symmetrically developed womanhood; the perfect poise of her figure is not more marked than the

perfect poise of her character. Not one
false note, not one exaggerated emphasis,
jars upon the harmony of body, soul, and
spirit. Confident, but entirely unassuming; serious, but without sadness; joyous,
but not to mirthfulness; eager, but without haste; she moves steadily forward
with steps timed to the rhythmic music
of the spheres. The child is no burden,
but a part of her very being. The two
are one in love, thought, and purpose.
Sharing the secret of his sacred calling,
the mother bears her son forth to meet
his glorious destiny.

Art can pay no higher tribute to Mary,
the Mother of Jesus, than to show her in
this phase of her motherhood. We sym-
pathize with her maternal tenderness,
lavishing fond caresses upon her child.
We go still deeper into her experience
when we see her bowed in sweet humility
before the cares and duties she is called

upon to assume.   But we are admitted to
the most cherished aspirations of her soul,
when we see her oblivious of self, carrying
her child forth to the service of humanity.
It is thus that she becomes one of his
" witnesses unto the people; " it is thus that
" all generations shall call her blessed."

BIBLIOGRAPHY.

MRS. ANNA JAMESON: The Legends of the Madonna. Boston, 1896.

CROWE AND CAVALCASELLE: History of Painting in Italy. London, 1864. History of Painting in North Italy. London, 1871. Titian: His Life and Times. London, 1877.

KUGLER: Handbook of the Italian Schools, revised by A. H. Layard. London, 1887. Handbook of the German, Flemish, and Dutch Schools, revised by J. A. Crowe. London, 1889.

MORELLI: Critical Studies of the Italian Painters. Translated by Constance Jocelyn Ffoulkes. London, 1892.

J. A. SYMONDS: Renaissance in Italy: The Fine Arts. New York, 1888.

WALTER II. PATER: Studies in the History of the Renaissance. London, 1873.

BERNHARD BERENSON: The Venetian Painters of the Renaissance. New York, 1894. The Florentine Painters of the Renaissance. New York, 1896.

KARL KÁROLY : A Guide to the Paintings of Florence.
London and New York, 1893. A Guide to the
Paintings of Venice. London and New York, 1895.
C. C. PERKINS: Tuscan Sculptors. London, 1864.
CAVALUCCI ET MOLINIER: Les Della Robbia: leur vie
et leur œuvre. Paris, 1884.
EUGENE MÜNTZ: Raphael. Translated by Walter
Armstrong. London, 1882.

INDEX OF ARTISTS.